Merry Christmas!
Louise Mandrell

To Nicole Mandrell Shipley,
an answer to a mother's prayers.
And to Clint and Rance Collins,
the godchildren who have
blessed my life beyond compare.
LOUISE

For my sons, Clint and Rance,
who have taught me that
a parent's smiles and tears
are the most precious
of all of God's gifts.
ACE

To all the children
who will touch this book,
may your childhood
be filled with love.
LOUISE AND ACE

Jonathan's Gifts

Jonathan's Gifts

Louise Mandrell and Ace Collins

Children's Holiday Adventure Series
Volume 16

THE SUMMIT GROUP

1227 West Magnolia, Suite 500, Fort Worth, Texas 76104

© 1992 by The Summit Group. All rights reserved.

This document may not be duplicated in any way without the expressed written consent
of the publisher. Making copies of this document, or any portion of it for any purpose
other than your own, is a violation of the United States copyright laws.

All rights reserved. Published 1992.

Printed in the United States of America.

92   10   9   8   7   6   5   4   3   2

Jacket and Book Design by Cheryl Corbitt

LIBRARY OF CONGRESS CATALOGING-IN-PUBLICATION DATA

Mandrell, Louise.

    Jonathan's Gifts / by Louise Mandrell and Ace Collins; illustrated by Mark Gale.

    p. cm. – (Holiday adventure series; v. 16)

    Summary: On a snowy Christmas Eve in the Ozark Mountains during the Depression, ten-
year-old Jonathan uses his savings to help a young couple in trouble and receives an unexpected
holiday surprise.

    ISBN 1-56530-012-2; $12.95

    [1. Christmas – Fiction. 2. Gifts – Fiction. 3. Depressions – 1929 – Fiction. 4. Ozark
Mountains – Fiction.] I. Collins, Ace. II. Gale, Mark, ill. III. Title. IV. Series: Mandrell, Louise.
Holiday adventure series; v. 16.

PZ7. M31254Jo 1992

[Fic] – dc20   92-31608

CIP

AC

Illustrated by Mark Gale

THE SUMMIT GROUP

The snow had been steadily falling
ever since sunrise.

The Ozark Mountains would be wrapped in a deep,
white blanket by tomorrow, Christmas Day. Most of the
people who lived in and around Ash Flat, Arkansas,
were inside warming themselves by pot-bellied stoves.
They were wrapping modest presents and decorating
freshly cut cedar trees with tinsel, homemade ornaments
and strings of popcorn as if to say that the hard times
of the 1930s could not take away their spirit or the joy
of the season.

Jonathan Worle had finished his chores early, and while his brothers and sisters played on an ice-covered pond, he had sneaked away and begun a four-mile walk to town. He was dressed in a hand-me-down green corduroy jacket, tattered work gloves, and dark rubber boots. A cotton toboggan was pulled down over his ears, and a homemade yellow scarf was wrapped about his neck. Yet, in spite of all this protection, the cold north wind still cut through him like a knife.

Beside Jonathan was his three-year-old sable and white collie. Laddie was the only thing of value the boy had ever owned. He was a show-quality dog that had been given to the Worles when their neighbors had moved to the city. The dog and Jonathan had taken to each other right away and soon became inseparable. Laddie went everywhere with Jonathan. Today, Laddie would rather have been sleeping in the warmth of the barn instead of out walking in the bitter cold. Yet, here he was, as always, by Jonathan's side.

Deep in a pocket of Jonathan's bib overalls, carefully wrapped in an old sock, was almost four dollars in small coins. The ten-year-old boy had worked all summer to earn this much money: piling rocks, carrying water to the men and women who worked in the fields, and chopping the weeds out of cotton patches. In September he had given Mart Carpenter, the owner of the general store, fifty cents as a down payment on four mono-grammed handkerchiefs and a small copper teapot. Mr. Carpenter had put them in the back room, and Jonathan had promised that he would finish paying for them before Christmas.

As the youngest of seven brothers and sisters, he had never before been able to buy gifts for his parents.

In the past he had just made a card at school and put it under the tree. But this year, he promised himself, he was going to give them the best presents that they had ever received. The closer he got to town, the more excited he became, just thinking about the look on his mother's face when she unwrapped the shiny copper kettle, and how pleased his father was going to be with those new handkerchiefs.

An hour later, he was within a mile of Ash Flat. Suddenly, Laddie caught a scent and bolted off the road. Jonathan paused and peered through the blinding snow for a few seconds, but trudged on into the wind. He knew that when the collie finished exploring he would catch up. But Laddie didn't come; the collie began to bark insistently.

"Laddie!" Jonathan called out. "I don't have time to play. Come on!"

The dog stayed where he was and kept barking.

Grudgingly, Jonathan left the road and waded through knee-deep snow toward the sound of Laddie's barking. Across the wide ditch he came upon the dog.

"Laddie," he hollered, "I'm getting cold. Let's go!"

Ignoring the boy, the dog shook the snow from his coat and rushed down the hill. Something told Jonathan to follow. When he got to the bottom he saw what Laddie had found. An old, worn Model T Ford had slid off the road and crashed down the hill. Only a large oak tree had kept it from running into the river. The front of the sedan had been mangled. Jonathan could see that the car would never run again.

Rushing to the passenger door, Jonathan wiped the snow from the window and looked inside. A man and woman were huddled in the front seat. Jonathan pounded on the glass, and the woman looked up, startled, but the man never moved.

"Oh, thank God!" the woman cried as she forced her door open. Jonathan saw that she was small, frail-looking, and about twenty. Even though she wore a large, heavy coat, he could tell that she was pregnant.

"Are you all right?" he asked.

Nodding her head, she replied, "I think I'll be fine, but my husband passed out a few minutes ago. He needs a doctor, quickly!"

Jonathan looked over at the man. Thanks to the cold, he could see the man's breath and knew that he was alive. Still, his face was very pale, and he had a large bump on his head.

"Listen," the boy told the woman, "Doc Billingsly lives about a mile up the road. I'll leave Laddie here, and I'll run to his house."

When she heard that Jonathan was leaving them, the woman looked frightened.

"Don't be afraid," Jonathan said. "Laddie will protect you, and I'll be back before you know it." Turning to the collie, he ordered, "Stay until I call you."

The dog's intelligent brown eyes showed that he understood. As the boy raced off and disappeared in a mass of white flakes, Laddie lay down on the far side of the crumpled car to wait there until the boy returned.

It was the longest mile Jonathan had ever run. The ice made the ground slippery, and the whirling snow kept him from seeing the road clearly. Although he fell more times than he could count, he continued to run. He knew he had to get the doctor in a hurry.

He was about halfway there when he heard a motor. In front of him a huge truck slowly emerged from the wall of white. When he saw it, Jonathan waved his arms wildly and jumped up and down in the middle of the road. At first the driver signaled for him to move. Then, seeing that the stubborn child was staying put, he came to a stop.

"Get out of my way, kid," he yelled as he rolled down the window.

Running up to the cab, Jonathan jumped on the running board and pleaded, "There was a wreck back down the road. There are people who are hurt. I need to hitch a ride to Doc Billingsly's."

"Where's he live?" the driver quickly asked.

"Ash Flat," Jonathan answered.

"Sorry," the driver responded, "I just went through there, and now I've got to get to Salem."

"Please," Jonathan begged. "It will take me at least a half an hour to get there in this weather, and that might be too late."

"Listen, kid," the driver replied, "try to understand this. If I don't get this load delivered to Salem I can't get paid, and if I don't get paid I won't have the money to buy my kid the baseball glove he wants for Christmas."

Jonathan was about to give up when a desperate idea came to him. "How much is the glove?"

"What?" the driver hollered over the roar of the motor.

"How much does the glove cost?" Jonathan repeated.

"Three dollars," came the terse response.

"I'll give you three dollars to take me to Doc's," he shouted.

"You got three dollars?" the surprised driver inquired.

"Yes, sir," the boy answered. "Now, please take me to Doc's."

When he arrived at the Billingsly's stone house, Jonathan was deeply relieved to see the doctor's green Model A Ford parked in the driveway. This meant that Doc was home. Digging into his pocket the boy retrieved his sock and counted out three dollars. Handing it to the

man, he opened the door, hopped down to the ground, and raced up the drive. Jumping onto the long porch, the boy knocked mightily on the wooden front door. He didn't stop pounding until a tall, middle-aged man with graying hair pulled open the door.

"All right, all right," Doc yelled. "I can hear you." He stared in disbelief at the snow-covered visitor and then asked, "Jonathan Worle, is that you? Come inside out of the cold. How did you get here?" His question was answered when he looked past the boy and saw the large truck using his driveway to turn around.

Shaking the snow from his coat, the trembling Jonathan grabbed the doctor's arm and gave it a pull.

"Doc!" he frantically exclaimed. "There has been a car wreck up on '63'. There's a man who's been pretty badly hurt. I found him . . . well, actually, Laddie did, and he needs you."

"OK, son," Doc answered in a calm voice. "Let me get my bag and coat, and we'll get in the car. Then you can take me back there. Do you need something to warm you up?"

"We don't have time!" Jonathan cried.

The Model A didn't like the cold weather any more than Doc did, and he had to step on the starter a half-dozen times before the engine caught. Once they got going, the car's tall wheels gave them enough clearance to avoid getting stuck in the snow. Within ten minutes they had arrived at the spot where Laddie had first charged off the road.

"Here it is!" Jonathan cried out.

"I don't see anything," Doc Billingsly answered as he surveyed the scene between the wiper's slow sweeps over the windshield.

"Down the hill," Jonathan answered. "Come on, I'll show you!"

After the doctor shut the car off, the two quickly piled out into the sharp, cruel wind. The doctor watched Jonathan race off across the ditch, stop, look around as if lost, and then cry out, "Laddie, Laddie!"

From out of nowhere a snow-covered mass of fur came bounding up to him. "Come on, Doc. Laddie will lead the way!" A moment later they had arrived at the wreck.

"I'm Doc Billingsly," the doctor explained as he opened the passenger door.

"I'm Mary Rhoads," the woman answered. "My husband's been badly injured!"

"How are *you* feeling?" Doc inquired.

"I'm cold," she answered, "but I'm going to be all right. It's Joe I'm worried about."

After performing a quick examination, the doctor reached into his bag and pulled out some smelling salts.

Holding the vial under the man's nose for a few seconds brought him around.

"Mr. Rhoads," the doctor explained as the man's eyes began to focus, "I'm a doctor, and we need to get you and your wife up to my car. Now tell me, besides your head, is there anything else that hurts?"

"No," the young man replied quietly.

"Good. Then I'm going to get you up the hill, and my young friend will assist your wife."

Jonathan helped the young woman out of the car and supported her as she waded through the foot-deep snow. Behind them, Doc Billingsly half-carried, half-dragged the still dizzy Joe Rhoads back toward his car. Laddie climbed through the snow along with them.

Opening the back door, Jonathan got Mary Rhoads settled in the car, and then ran back down to help Doc and Joe. Putting Joe's arm around his shoulder, Jonathan helped Doc pull the hurting man. As soon as they got him in the back seat, Jonathan and Laddie jumped up front with the doctor.

"You hang on," Doc called out. "We're probably going to slip and slide some." He lowered his voice and looked over at Jonathan. "Boy, you tell me if either one of those folks starts to look poorly."

The Model A's engine caught the first time, and the group slowly headed down the almost impassable highway. As they eased through drifts and over patches of ice, Jonathan kept his eyes trained on the two people in the back seat.

"We sure do thank you," Joe acknowledged as the boy's eyes met his own. "We would have died if you hadn't found us."

"Laddie found you," Jonathan answered. "He deserves the credit."

"But you got the doctor," Mary interjected.

"It wasn't really anything," the boy replied, embarrassed.

"Where are you folks from?" Doc inquired.

"We used to live in West Virginia," Joe answered. "Times got tough, and I lost my job as a store manager when the mine closed. Folks just weren't buying enough for the owner to keep the store open. With the baby coming and no money, I knew I had to find something quick. I heard they were hiring out west, so we sold what we had and bought a car."

"It's been tough," Mary explained. "The car kept breaking down, and we had to use more of our savings than we thought. Now, with the car wrecked, I don't know what we'll do."

Jonathan heard the pain in the woman's voice. It seemed terribly sad to be that hopeless on Christmas Eve.

"Well, here we are," Doc announced as he pulled off the highway into his lane. "Now, as soon as I get this thing stopped, we'll take you inside and patch you up."

Jonathan and Laddie waited by the roaring pot-bellied stove as the doctor examined his new patients. Sitting on the stone hearth, the boy pondered. He had spent three dollars, and now he had just one dollar left. That wasn't enough to purchase even one of the gifts he had picked out for his parents. He'd just have to go to the store, find something very cheap, and make do. The more he thought about it, the more disappointed he became.

"Jonathan," the doctor whispered as he came back into the room.

"Yes, Doc?" the boy answered.

"These folks don't have any money at all. It seems that they haven't even eaten anything since yesterday. And now Mrs. Rhoads is going to have her baby. I can take care of that problem, but I might need a couple of things from Mart Carpenter's store. Can you brave the cold one more time and get them for me?"

Nodding his head, Jonathan reached for his coat. As he did, Doc handed him a list.

"Give this to Mr. Carpenter," he explained. "Just a few things I might need if we have any problems with the delivery. He'll put it on my bill, so don't worry about paying for it. Now, don't tarry."

Taking a deep breath, Jonathan opened the front door and was greeted once again by the frigid north wind. A thermometer on the porch read fifteen degrees, but with the wind and snow it seemed even colder. With Laddie by his side, he fought his way down the road to Ash Flat. The short half-mile walk seemed to take a very long time.

Carpenter's store carried everything from clothes to food. It was also a central meeting place for everyone in the area. When Jonathan arrived, there was a large crowd of folks picking up fruit, candy, and gifts and swapping stories about hunting and politics.

As they approached the building, the dog left the boy's side. Laddie knew he couldn't go in, so he found a dry spot under the building's porch. After stamping his snow-caked boots, Jonathan pushed on the large, glass-paned wooden door. He had no more than gotten it open when the store owner's booming voice greeted him.

"Young Mr. Worle," Mart announced, "I know why you braved the snow to come see me. I have what you want right here behind the counter."

Shaking his head sadly, Jonathan approached the heavy-set man and said almost in a whisper, "No, I won't be buying them now. I lost most of my money. I'm sorry. Maybe you can sell them to someone else."

Reaching into his coat pocket, the boy pulled out a crumpled piece of paper. "Doc needs these things," he said as he handed the shopkeeper the list.

Seeing that the boy was close to tears, the man didn't ask any questions. He just walked into his back room where he kept the few medical supplies he stocked.

As he waited for the order to be filled, Jonathan looked around the store hoping to find something inexpensive for his parents. Everything he saw cost much too much.

"What's going on out at Doc's?" Mr. Carpenter asked as he came back into the room.

"A couple was in a car wreck," Jonathan explained. "The man got banged up a little, and now the lady's having a baby. They seem like real nice folks. They're from out east. He lost his job when a store closed down. Now they have no money, and their car is wrecked. I guess Christmas is going to be real sad for them, even with the baby."

"Here's the stuff Doc wanted," Mr. Carpenter said as he handed Jonathan a small sack. "You say they're nice folks?"

"Real nice," Jonathan answered. Then he got an idea. Pointing at a small stuffed animal hanging high on a far wall, the boy asked, "How much is that bear?"

"A dollar," the store owner replied in surprise.

"I'll take it," Jonathan answered as he dug for his money. Counting it out, he put the now empty sock back in his pocket and headed toward the door.

"Jonathan," Mr. Carpenter called out after him, "I'd give you a ride home, but I haven't got anybody to watch the store. Mr. Jenkins got a job working in Oklahoma in the oil fields. I need to find someone to replace him. . . . You say that this is a nice couple?"

Jonathan had just reached the door. "Yes, yes they are. And this man really needs a job."

"Jonathan," Mr. Carpenter spoke as he crossed the store. "I never hire people without checking them out. But I've got to go down to Little Rock next week, and I need somebody quick. So, just what makes you so sure about this guy?"

"I don't know," the boy replied. "It's just a feeling."

Looking into the boy's light green eyes, the store owner thought things over for a few moments, smiled, and said, "Well, it's Christmas. You tell your friend to come see me in the next few days if he's really looking for a place to work. Tell him there's an apartment over the store and he, his wife, and the baby can live there. I'll make sure they have enough supplies until he gets his first paycheck. Like I said, it's Christmas. By the way, what are their names?"

"Mr. and Mrs. Rhoads," Jonathan replied. "Joe and Mary Rhoads."

The trip back to the doctor's house was much easier. The snow had let up, the wind had died down, and Jonathan knew that he had glad tidings to bring to this unfortunate couple.

"That's wonderful!" Joe exclaimed when Jonathan told him what the store owner had said. "I'll get over there just as soon as I can. Mary will be so excited. We didn't have anyone we could turn to and no hope, and now we have a home for our new child. We can never repay you."

"I didn't do much," Jonathan shrugged. "I was going to town anyway, and Mr. Carpenter needs the help."

Just then the doctor came back into the room.

"Is everything all right?" Joe asked.

"Everything is fine," the doctor replied. Turning to Jonathan he asked, "Did you get the things I needed?"

"Sure did," Jonathan answered as he handed the doctor the sack. "And I got this for the baby," he said a little shyly, holding out the small stuffed bear. "Everyone needs something special at Christmas. Now, I've got to get on home. We're having our Christmas tonight."

A few hours later, the Worle family gathered in their small living room. Tom Worle, Jonathan's father, read to his children from the Bible, led them in a few carols, and finally signaled for the oldest son, Lige, to begin handing out the presents.

As his family laughed and talked, Jonathan could only sit in the corner thinking about the way things should have been. He felt miserable. He had let his parents down. He had nothing to give them.

"Somebody's coming," Audrey suddenly cried out.

"Who would be coming here on Christmas Eve?" Mr. Worle asked.

"It's Doc," Beulah announced as she peered through the window.

"Nobody's been sick," Mr. Worle mused. "I wonder what he wants?"

A few minutes later, after greetings had been exchanged, the man who had delivered all the Worle children found a chair by the stove. As he sat down, he placed a big sack in his lap.

"I came up here tonight," Doc began, "to bring something that was left in town. By the way, did Jonathan tell you about the adventure he had today?"

"No," Mrs. Worle answered. "He hasn't said much of anything since he got back home. As a matter of fact, he didn't even tell any of us where he had been. He just said it was a surprise that didn't work out."

"Well, then," the doctor answered, "I'll tell you."

And he told them all about the Rhoads family, and the car accident, and the trip through the snowstorm.

"And," he concluded happily, "the baby came! It's a boy – and they've named him Jonathan."

Looking up, an embarrassed Jonathan smiled, his eyes sparkling. He felt proud. His family crowded around to congratulate him, and the doctor smiled and continued with his story.

"After the baby came, I had to get to town to look in on a few folks. On the way out, I looked in my mailbox for last-minute Christmas cards.

"In the box I found three dollars and a note from the truck driver. He asked me to give it to the boy who had hitched a ride, and tell the boy that he was sorry he accepted it. Well, I put the money in my pocket. When I stopped at Carpenter's, I told Mart Carpenter my story, and he gave me these two packages that he said he had been saving for Jonathan.

"So, Tom and Ann, I believe these things are for you." And the doctor handed Jonathan's parents two neatly wrapped packages.

As the two opened the boxes, the doctor walked over to Jonathan and handed him an envelope. Looking inside, the boy found three brand-new one dollar bills.

The doctor whispered, "I didn't have a chance to pay you for running that errand for me."

"But Doc," Jonathan protested.

"No, you earned it," he answered, "and a lot more. Mr. Carpenter, the Rhoadses, and I all agree. This year you showed us the real spirit of the season. Merry Christmas, Jonathan, and, from all of us, thank you for your special gifts!"

Though no one actually knows the date
of Christ's birth, in most countries Christmas
has been celebrated on or about
December 25 since the fourth century.
Ironically, this, the most cherished
of American holidays, was not universally marked
until the second half of the nineteenth century.
In fact, throughout the early 1700s,
the Puritans outlawed all celebrations
associated with the day and even ordered
all shops to remain open.
Now Americans combine the story
of the birth of Christ with traditions from cultures
worldwide to make Christmas a time of
family, giving, music, thanks,
and thoughts of peace.